Ladybird Talkabout Books are designed for young children to share with someone older. A child who doesn't read yet can enjoy looking at the books alone, but the greatest pleasure and benefit will come from talking about the pictures. Each book is intended to prompt conversation, to encourage observation and awareness, and to stimulate vocabulary and the imagination. The simple text will lead naturally to discussion of the pictures. As you look at the book together, don't hurry. Allow the child to associate freely, and let yourself do the same. You may be delighted to discover that you both find new things to explore and talk about with every fresh reading.

Talkabout Home deals with a basic subject in children's lives. The pictures show everyday objects and situations familiar to all children. The pictures also provide opportunities to reinforce basic skills like counting and color and shape identification, and to discuss such concepts as opposites. For example, on the first two pages you can talk about short and tall, high and low, big and small. In the picture on pages 8 and 9, you can count the blocks and find all the round things. And on the "Tell the story" pages, the child may notice that the car is red, the moving van orange, and the girl's overalls blue.

LADYBIRD BOOKS, INC.
Auburn, Maine 04210 U.S.A.
© LADYBIRD BOOKS LTD 1988
Loughborough, Leicestershire, England

Printed in England

TALKABOUT

Home

by ELLEN RUDIN
illustrated by LINDA WELLER

Ladybird Books

Talk about different kinds of homes.

Which one is something like your home?

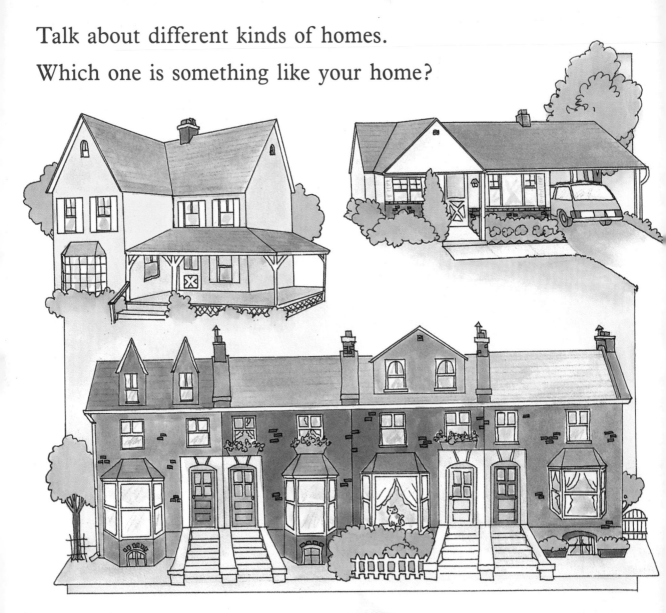

What are these rooms called?

Talk about this room.

ABCDEFG
HIJKLMNO
PQRST
UVWXYZ

What is happening in the pictures?

This home has a basement.

This home has an attic.

Match each thing
with the black shape
that is like it.

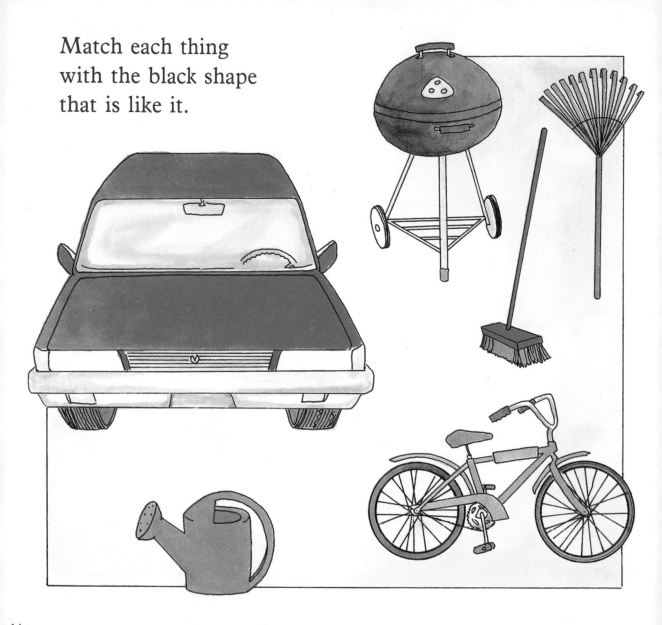

Talk about housework.

Talk about the yard.

17

Company is here!
What could be
in the box?

What is each person doing?

Find something silly in each room.

20

Talk about staying home.

What do you think is inside?

Tell the story.

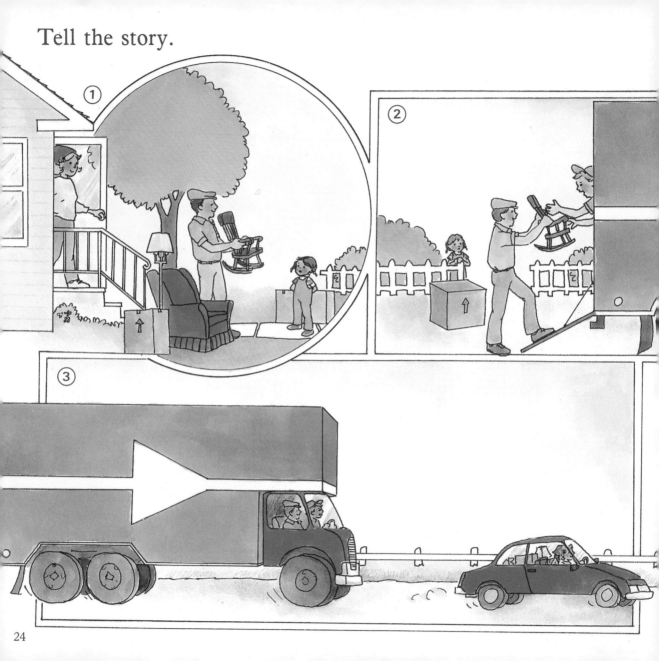

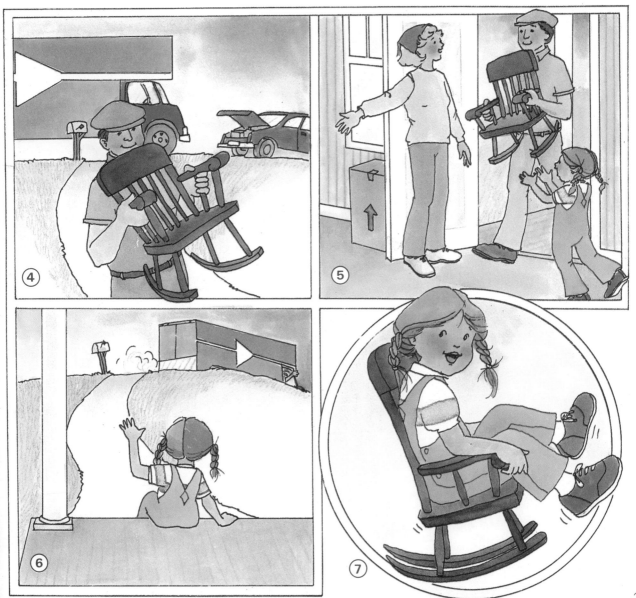

Talk about playing house.